Janet Logie Robertson

Our Holiday Among the Hills

Janet Logie Robertson

Our Holiday Among the Hills

ISBN/EAN: 9783337288075

Printed in Europe, USA, Canada, Australia, Japan

Cover: Foto ©Andreas Hilbeck / pixelio.de

More available books at **www.hansebooks.com**

Our Holiday
Among the Hills

BY

JAMES AND JANET LOGIE ROBERTSON

WILLIAM BLACKWOOD AND SONS
EDINBURGH AND LONDON
MDCCCLXXXII

THIS level turnpike road we daily tread,
With its high hedges hiding from our view
The features of the land we journey through,
Inspires—not dreariness alone—but dread.
Let but a cloud eclipse the blue o'erhead,
A thicket dull the distance, or a new
And unexpected turning change the hue
And current of our hopes—and peace is fled!
—Then let us leave the road awhile, my friend!
How all my being wakes, and, pulsing, thrills
To this pure mountain air!   As we ascend,
How sink to insignificance our ills!
Gladness and gloom in perfect beauty blend—
Life is a lovely landscape FROM THE HILLS !

THE shepherd *Moses* ON THE HILLSIDE *saw*
A green buss bleezin', bleezin' aye awa';
Nae reck rase up, nae ashes fell adoun,
There was nae sough o' fire, nae cracklin' soun';
But clear an' constant was the steady flame,
An' unconsum'd the buss, an' aye the same.

Ye needna doot the shepherd glowred wi' awe
At sic a strange suspension o' the law
That dooms to swift destruction barn or byre,
Biggin' or buss that's grippit ance by fire.
In this he saw the presence o' his God,
An' felt the grund was holy whaur he trod.

That selfsame miracle does yet appear:
We see it i' the spring o' every year,
When whin an' bonnier broom are fairly bloom'd,
An', wavin', burn the same an' unconsum'd
—But unregardit o' baith man an' woman,
Quite unregardit, for the sicht's sae common!
They see't a' gate—alangs' the public way,
In gowden beauty bleezin', bleezin' aye,
Till every hill-tap, craig, an' spritty knowe
Owre Scotland braid like flamin' altars lowe!
Yet wha draws near wi' reverential feet?
Or is there ane that worships but to see't?
Nae thocht is theirs that God's within the buss,
Or that the grund is holy brightened thus!

CONTENTS.

PART I.—SONGS.

PART V.— HORACE IN HOMESPUN : OR, THE FRIENDS AND FORTUNES OF HUGHIE HALIBURTON, A SHEPHERD OF THE OCHILS.

PART I.—SONGS.

WITHIN THE SKJÆRGAARD.

HERE, in my little boat embayed,
   Unseen but safe, I lie,
And watch, beyond the headland's shade,
   The mighty ships go by.

Full swells the blue, the brimming tide
   Sparkles the sunshine clear;
And to and fro, and free they glide,
   And far away, and near.

To them the sweep of all the sea,
   And all the sweep of sky;—
This little boat and bay to me
   And room enough have I

A

Yet still—though hill, and head, and cliff
My narrow welkin shear—
To witness from my rocking skiff
The star of eve appear;

And still—though in the sheltering lee
And shadow of the shore—
To feel the tides of the great sea
I will not venture o'er !

———o———

THE MUSE OF POETRY.

They have brought her into the town:
Can you wonder she is become pale ?

I.

THEY enticed her away from the mountain,
Where lightly she frolickt a fawn,
From the truth of her face in the fountain,
From peace, and the blessing of dawn.

II.

She had run with the light step of childhood
O'er moorland, and meadow, and lea;
And hers was the range of the wild wood,
Where boldly she sang, and was free.

III.

In the shade of the hazel she rested,
  She couched among wild flowers and fern;
But the stars only knew where she nested—
  The stars, and the high-sailing ern.

IV.

She was free as the wind, and as froward ;
  And fresh as the rose, and as fair ;
And her speech, if outspoken, had *no* word
  That truth did not wish to be there.

V.

But they saw her, the beaux of the city,
  And proffered her praise, and a crown ;
And she yielded—the more was the pity—
  She yielded, and went to the town.

VI.

And the grace of her virginhood vanished,
  And all the sweet dreams of her home ;
And her friends were forbidden, or banished,
  And freedom to rest or to roam.

VII.

They had crowned her the Siren of Singers
  —Yet never a song sang she now ;

For the crown that was gold in their fingers
Was lead, and a load on her brow.

VIII.

And her cheek became bloomless and pallid,
The sparkle was lost from her eye;
—All in vain to her aidance she rallied
Her mem'ries : they came but to sigh.

IX.

Can they blame her, those men without pity,
For cheeks that are haggard and pale?
For they lured her away to the city,
And sought of her song to have sale.

X.

Oh, the kiss and the clasp of the moonlight
Lay softer by far on her brow
Than the gyve—though it looks so like sunlight—
Which presses so hard on it now!

XI.

Can they wonder, her prestige recounting,
Her voice has been silent so long,
Who enticed her away from the fountain
And source of all solace and song?

ENCHANTED GROUND.

I.

STILL by the banks of the stream I stand
  That borders the land of Truth ;
The skies are blue, and the winds are bland
  And blow from the shores of Youth.
Rich are the blooms in the amber air,
  And the forest favours green,
And aye the wings of an angel fair
  Flash through the golden scene !
And I hear the bells of Hope that seem
  To sprinkle the air with sound,
Now far away in the depths of a dream,
  Now clashing all around !

II.

Flow on, flow ever, Fancy dear !
  · Sweet stream I love so well !
Blend with the tones I yet do hear
  From Hope's air-belfried bell !
And live, ye winds of youthful years !
  Still, fostering, let me find,
Though on my body age appears,
  Your freshness on my mind !

And still be thy bright wings displayed,
  Where sometimes I may see
And feel their magic, loveliest maid !
  Angelic Poesie !

—————o—————

A MORNING LOVE-SONG.

I.

WOODBINE that clingest fair
  At my love's casement—
    Sweet be thy savour
      For sake of her bower !
Blossom that swingest there
  High from the basement—
    Oh for the favour
      Thou hast at this hour !

II.

Swallow that wingest the
  Fleetest of small birds—
    Thou at her waking
      Canst see how she seems !
Laverock that singest the
  Sweetest of all birds—
    Thou at day-breaking
      Canst break on her dreams !

III.

Morning that flingest bright
  Gold in the fountain—
    Oh with thy radiance
      T'enrapture her eye !
Breeze that upspringest light
  On the green mountain—
    Oh with thy fragrance
      T'enfold her and die !

———o———

WILLIAM'S BRIDAL.

".May happiness be in that ha',
  And bliss be in that bower,
And Fortune's golden treasures fa'
  Upon them every hour ! "
Oh never since the world began,
  And love on life had sway,
Shone sweeter face or fairer sun
  Than did that bridal day !
"May happiness be in their bower,
  And bliss be in their ha'—"
It was the worship o' the hour,
  The wish o' anc an' a'.

And never cloud aboon them hung
　That sunny bridal day;
And William's bride-elect was young
　And blithesome as the May !
Oh he was brave, and she was braw,
　And birds aboon them sang ;
Baith boor and baron blessed the twa—
　And wha would wished them wrang ?
—Yet William mounts the weary stairs
　To sit and sigh his lane,
And a' thae bonnie hopes o' theirs
　Are blastit, ane an' ane !

————o————

VOX AMORIS. ˙

　THE birds are singing,
　The woods are ringing,
　　　And hark ! . . . hark !
They're laughing, the waves o' the sea !
　　　—Merrily pipe, thou mounting lark !
The girl I love loves me !

　The sun is glancing,
　The waves are dancing,

And look ! . . . look !
They're smiling, the flowers o' the lea !
   —Merrily laugh, thou prattling brook !
The girl I love loves me !

——*o*——

CRAIGIE GLEN.

THE hazel's in her summer green ;
   The wakening woods, so fair
With honeysuckle and with gean—
   It's oh that I was there !

I see as in a haunting dream
   The white anemones
Dim-shivering by the dark glen-stream,
   Amid the gloom of trees.

And boyhood's days dawn back again,
   And boyhood's thoughts return,
As when I roamed in Craigie Glen,
   And fished in Craigie burn.

Oh days o' joy, with little pain,
   Oh happy thoughts were these !
—They come like fragrance o'er the brain,
   Or long-lost melodies !

How humble were the highest hopes
  That heaved my bosom then !
—My gold was on the primrose slopes
  Wide-scattered through the glen !

Now passions rage, and anger glooms
  —But sinless days were these,
And passionless as the pale blooms
  Of the anemones.

And these in dream break in once more
  Upon the cares of men—
Like voices from a fading shore
  We'll never see again !

Oh to indulge the boyish mood,
  With but a boyish care !
My heart is in the summer wood
  —My feet will soon be there !

———0———

THE DAWN OF LOVE.

A YOUNG god met me yesternight
  On the scented sun-dried hill,
A young god kissed me on the height
  And my lips are burning still ;

And it's oh ! it's oh !
The morning glow
  Is pulsing through my frame !
And it's oh ! it's oh !
For the Lapland snow
  To cool the burning flame !

He pressed a soft red lip to mine
  On the moonlit mountain height,
He touched me but with his lips divine
  And vanished from my sight !
    But it's oh ! it's oh !
    The morning glow
      Is pulsing through my frame !
    And it's oh ! it's oh !
    For the Lapland snow
      To cool the burning flame !

—*o*—

BLUE-BELLS.

THOUGHTS too tender to be spoken
  Flood my fancy gazing there,
Where they, from their kindred broken,
    Deck that mountain bare !

—Blue-bells ! crowding in the crevice,
　　What a trustful look ye wear,
On the rough breast of Ben Nevis
　　　Leaning, free of care !

Bonnie when the sunshine glances
　　Like a hope when hopes are rare,
On the cliff your shadow dances
　　　—Bonnie past compare !

Joyous life to you's a duty,
　　Tossing freely, tossing fair,
All your blue tumultuous beauty,
　　　On the billowy air !—

Dream of Beauty ! be about me,
　　How or wheresoe'er I fare ;
What were Earth—were Life without thee
　　　But a bleak despair ?

———*o*———

TO MAISRIE.

IF you would deign on me to smile,
　　And dare to go with me,
I'd bear you to a fairy isle
　　Lies lonely 'mid the sea.

And there afar from scenes of pain
And hid from human view,
We'd practise whether of the twain
Was happier—I or you !

————o————

IN A HOLLOW OF THE HILLS.

In a hollow of the hills,
  Green as Eden round me,
By the babble of soft rills
  Slumber sweet had bound me.

As I lay in bliss entranced,
  Faces, fair and smiling,
On me in a vision glanced
  —All my soul beguiling.

Come again, dear angel-dream !
  Never to be spoken !
What though pleasure only seem ?
  Though the charm be broken ?

He with wisdom were at strife
  That would "lichtlie" dreaming ;
Half the joys of waking life,
  —What are they but seeming ?

FLOWER-FLAME!

ONE touch of Summer's golden torch
   And all the land's a-bloom!
—The mountain-ridge, the garden-porch
   With roses burn, and broom!

See where it runs along the lane,
   Flees waving o'er the waste,
Expatiates on the mountain plain
   With purple-spreading haste—

It is the fairy floral fire
   Down-flashed from Summer's sun,
Keen-quivering with fulfilled desire
   And liberty begun!

It leaps the grey towers of the wood,
   And bounds from branch to bough,
And radiance, ripe and many-hued,
   Consumes their gloom! And now

It is the fairy forest-bowers
   With Summer's lamps a-glow!
It is the dawn, the day of flowers
   With every bud a-blow!

—ONE stroke of Winter's leaden mace
  Amid the Summer's fire,
And down the bright flames drop apace,
  Dull, deaden, and expire !

They vanish from the blackened hill,
  And from the woodland walk,
They drop into the droning rill
  From off the barren stalk !

Sobs the lone wind—for ne'er a bloom
  Of all he kissed remains !
It is the ghoulish land of gloom
  Drenched with December rains !

—Eternal Summer ! from thy heights
  Reach down thy torch, we pray !
The world is cold without thy lights.
  —Or come thyself, and stay !

——*o*——

THE WALL-FLOWER ON THE WALL.

Soft the moonlight's silvery fall
On the ruined castle wall,
Low the wind's complaining tone
Round each worn and wasted stone !

Here of yore at gloaming-fall,
Shadows on the moonlit wall,
Youth and Beauty wandered twining,
While the Star of Hope was shining !

Then, oh then, sweet love was all !—
Castles rose at Fancy's call,
Music filled th' enchanted air,
Faery blossoms flourished fair !

Softly may the moonlight fall
On the Wall-flower on the wall !
Long and low the wind complain
—Love can ne'er be here again !

———o———

THE LOVER'S WALK.

THE sunset fires of evening glow
 Behind a gathering cloud,
And winds that from the norlan' blow
 Go past me piping loud.
But down by the meadow, and over the burn,
 And up by the witch's tree,
With many a traverse and many a turn
 My path this night must be !

Between me and the Druid stone
  A hare scuds o'er the grass ;
A cushat, with contented moan,
  Upbraids me as I pass.
But through the dark planting, and out on the
    moss,
  And over the benty lea,
With wall to leap, and water to cross,
  My path this night shall be !

The moon looks up with frightened glower,
  Dim-glimmering on the night ;
And what is that by the haunted tower?
  —My girl in ghostly white !
My troubles are over, my travels are done,
  The fears of the mid-mirk flee ;
The girl I love, and the only one,
  —She's true to her tryst with me !

———*o*———

THE FISHER.

THE fisher lights his evening pipe
    And steers his boat to shore ;
His wife now from the window looks,
    Now waits him at the door.

B

Oh low may be the fisher's life,
　And small and poor his store,
But large his love for that dear wife
　Waits for him at the door.

The sunset paves his path with gold
　—Now what could heart have more?
Heaven smiles upon him at the sea,
　And human love on shore!

———o———

THE TRYSTING-TREE.

THEIR shadows to the hills return,
　The sheep are in the pen,
And there's a gean by Craigie-burn
　Is scenting all the glen.

Oh braw the birk, and tall the fir,
　And rich the rowan-tree,
And sweet the lilac's lavender
　—But aye the gean for me!

And I to see that bonnie tree
　Would walk a mile and ten,
And after biding there awee
　Walk blithely back again

Yet not for bonnie blossoms white,
  Nor graceful girlish air
So lovely in the dusky light,
  I call the gean-tree fair.

The dear, delightful, darling charm
  That makes me praise it so,
God and good angels keep from harm !
  —But *what*, you must not know !

———*o*———

THE KNIGHT AND THE LADY.

THE knight rides merrily forth to fight--
  Oh but the birds sing cheerily !
The lady weeps from morn till night
  While the rain falls wearily.

The knight wins love and high renown—
  Oh but the birds sing cheerily !
The lady's tears still wimple down
  As the rain falls wearily.

The knight comes back all gay of heart—
  Oh but the birds sing cheerily !
The lady in mirth must bear her part
  Though the rain falls wearily.

The knight he knows his fame is spread—
Oh but the birds sing cheerily !
The lady knows that his love is dead,
And the rain falls wearily.

PART II.—SCENES.

OUTWARD BOUND.

Reddas incolumem, precor,
Et serves animæ dimidium meæ.
— HOR., Car. 3, Lib. I.

I.

SHE speeds through southern seas ;
　And William in the bow
—His white hair by the steady breeze
　Blown forward on his brow—
Sees other scenes than Scottish trees
　And Scottish burnies now.

II.

Forward he seems to lean—
　As if with eager eyes

To anticipate the future scene
That far before him lies
Beyond the line that sweeps between
The ocean and the skies.

III.

What marvels lay aside
Their mystery to him !
What famous islets are descried
On the horizon dim !   ·
What constellations o'er him slide !
What monsters past him swim !

IV.

Leviathan at play
Tempests the weltering brine ;
The Southern Cross redeems the day
With radiancy divine ;
And on yon rock Napoleon lay
After his great decline !

V.

We traced, and traced again,
Schoolboys, with knitted brow,
Upon one atlas with a pen
The track of that ship's prow :
—*I* had the fuller knowledge then,
He has the ampler now.

VI.

Down the blue hemisphere,
   White sail ! to Table Bay,
For sake of one whom we hold dear,
   Glide steadily, we pray—
We twenty, in the hamlet here,
   Whose hearts thou bear'st away !

——*o*——

SUNSET ON THE LOMONDS.

SEE where into the sunset far
   The terraced mountains rise,
The cresset of a single star
   Just o'er them in the skies !
   Oh that to me a dove's meek eyes'
     And snow-white wings were given,
To reach yon hills and realise
     The calm they have from Heaven !
My soul is o'er the Vale of Leven,
     (Though here in streets I stray)
Till fades the holy golden even ;
     —The wish, too, dies away !

Alas for earth, that all it may
   Is but a mood in me !
And that when Heaven withdraws its ray
   The mood should·cease to be !

——*o*——

OUR DRIVE.

THE toll-road we left where a by-way
   Leaves room for a burnie between,
And now we look out on the highway
   From under an awning of green.

The bees in the cherry-tree o'er us
   Hum low, and are happy by stealth,
While hither and thither before us
   Flaunt coach-loads of fashion and wealth.

They're glancing and prancing, and feather
   And ribbon are sweeping the sky
—We sit in our arbour together
   And smilingly let them go by !

For we too are rich, and we know it,
   In health and in hope and in brains ;
And hold with the old Hebrew poet
   —Earth ours, and the joys it contains.

We, too, by the laws that o'er-rule us,
    Career it as grand as the great,
Our horses the forces that pull us,
    And earth our Quadriga of State !

Away in a curve that encloses
    The golden abode of the sun,
Through snowflakes, and raindrops, and roses,
    The steeds of our universe run !

How swiftly the wheels are revolving !
    How smoothly we're bowling along !
—Come, Janet ! I hope you're resolving
    To honour our drive with a song !

While I, with my heel on a pansy,
    And thyme in a bank at my back,
Will finger the reins with the fancy
    Of keeping our steeds in the track !

———o———

HOLIDAYS.

ONCE more, once more again
    On me, from city cares who fly,
    Lochleven, like a loving eye,
    Looks round the shoulder of the hills ;

And all life's artificial ills
Pass from me with their pain !

The smoke *will* leave a stain ;
  In absence of the cleansing shower
  The dust *will* dim the freshest flower :
  Happy the heart on whom the dust
  Of active life (for blow it must)
Grows not a thing in grain !

Nor are those ills in vain :
  They come upon our passions here
  Like winter rigours on the year—
  The purer are the daisies' dyes
  When Spring comes round, bluer the skies,
And welcomer the rain !

To some the breezy main ;
  To some the moors and burns ; to some·
  Who cannot go, sweet thoughts will come ;
  To me—enfranchisement from ills
  When gleams, as now, between the hills
Lochleven o'er the plain.

CASTLE GLOOM.

THE hand of Time, O Castle Gloom !
  Will soon be thy undoing ;
The *Mene Mene* of thy doom
  Is written on thy ruin !

What though the Ochils round thee stand,
  A bulwark firm and fast? ,
Thy strength is as the broken sand,
  Thy pride of power is past.

And of thy walls, to dust decayed,
  The rain has made a mould
Which feeds the saddening nettle-blade,
  Or wall-flower flecked with gold.

The mountain-ash with berries red
  Looks through thy windows high,
And rain upon thy floors is shed
  From rain-clouds passing by.

Still brawls the Sorrow round thy base
  To join his brother Care ;
—Oh, ill-advised they chose the place
  Who reared thy fabric there !

Ill-chosen was the place, the hour,
  Ill-omened was the name;
The sun even in meridian power
  Glooms on thy rugged frame!

—YET once, ere time completes thy doom,
  Thy halls with joy shall ring
Frightening the dreary birds of gloom
  That to thy corners cling.

For in thy topmost tower to-night
  Two hearts, made one in tune,
With Hymen's torches burning bright
  Light up the honeymoon.

And from thy topmost window-seat,
  When next the sun has shone,
His smile responsive smiles shall meet,
  More cheerful than his own!

——*o*——

MY WINDOW.

WHERE gold laburnum hangs in fringe
  And fragrant lilacs blow,
Where resting rays with rosy tinge
  Suffuse the hawthorn's snow,

Through elm-trees high in pride that stand
  With heads that pierce the skies,
My window gazes on the land
  That low before it lies.

Fair cultured fields in youthful bloom,
  Whose freshness glads the eye,
With here and there a grateful gloom
  Of forest dense and high,
With here and there a white highroad
  By March winds bleached and clean,
And thousand gleams of water strewed
  At random in between ;—

In terraces they slope away
  To meet reflected sky—
The deep blue waters of the bay
  That clear and tranquil lie.
The far horizon's line of light,
  The sunny, open sea,
The distant sails that glimmer white—
  How glad, and young, and free !

THE CATARACT.

SEE where he bursts in beauty bar and lock
  In a fierce haste to wed with her below,
  The gentle Elv, that steals with rippling flow
Along the deep-sunk dale ! With what a shock
His feet alight on this pink granite block !
  And how, half-stunned, he staggers to and fro,
  Compelled to pause, yet passionate to go,
Till, steadying all his strength, he shoots the
    rock !

The hazel coppice and a belt of pine
  Receive him next after his madman's bound ;
Yet still I see his great eyes, questing, shine
  Between the branches ; and I hear the sound
Of one whose lip is near some joy divine,
  Broken, and low, and last in rapture drowned.

———0———

CASTLE DESOLATE.

ON broken wall and fallen stone
  Are grass and lichen growing,
And winds around the courtyard moan
  Where bugles once were blowing !

And grey Oblivion's eyeless face
  Looks blankly through the grating
Where ladies once with witching grace
  Smiled to their knights in waiting !

And kaes and starlings build and breed
  Where social fires were roaring,
And from the donjon, choked with weed,
  A lark aloft is soaring.

———o———

WINTER : AN ELEGY.

I.

I LOOK from my lonely window
  Over the snowy plain—
A hearse and a handful of mourners
  Are creeping through the rain.
The flowers are dead and departed,
  The memory of Summer is gone,
Song from the lark, and the lark from heaven,
  —And the day drags on !

II.

My soul looks out from its grating,
  And sees without a sigh

The funeral train of youthful hopes
  Mournfully pass by.
Health, and the joy of existence,
  And the faiths that wont to be,
And love are dead and departing
  —It's winter with me !

———*o*———

THE VOICES OF NORWAY.

THE cataract thundering from the airy rock,
  Or shouting through the forest wild and free ;
  The river roaring onward to the sea,
Defiant of all craft to bind or block
Its loose unshackled strength ; the thunder-
      shock,
  Echoed in silence round the blasted tree ;
  And the black eagle screaming in his glee
Above the storm, which his strong wings be-
      mock :

—*These* are old Norway's voices : not the shrill
  Whistle of steam-car jarring down the street,
Nor clang of factory-bell, nor clank of mill
  Banging and beating to a fever-heat
Of madness blood and brain ; but Nature still
  Inhabits here, and men sit at her feet !

SUMMER ON THE LOMOND.

THE silver mists of morning rise
 Obedient to the sun,
And lo! the Lomond—to my eyes
Of all the hills that kiss the skies
 The dearest fairest one.

To Alps or Andes let them hie
 Who slight the hills at home—
To Alps and Andes let them fly:
With freer step will you and I
 Upon the Lomond roam.

Its ample upland lawns be ours,
 Forsaken yet so fair;
Its braes, its burnies, and its flowers,
Its long calm summer pastoral hours,
 And its ethereal air!

Oh sweet is love at eventide
 In green suburban lane!
But on the Lomond—time is wide,
And life is love, and glorified,
 And Eden back again!

C

IN ORWELL ACRE.

" Sui Vitam Innocuam per Plurima Lustra
Peregit Pace Diu Gaudens Hic Tumulatus
Obit Robertus Paterson—Mortem Subiit Ann.
Dom. 1669, Ætatis Vero 97."

FORGET-ME-NOTS around the table grow
  —Nature's unconscious satire, for indeed,
What with the weather, wear of time, and
    weed,
We scarce make out the little that we know
Of Robert Paterson who sleeps below.
    Patience and spell !   And now at last we read
  In Latin old the meagre facts we need
To set us thinking of the long ago.

Here was a patriarchal length of life
  That ran its peaceful course to ninety-seven,
Begun when Shakespeare played, nor thought
    of wife,
  (A little tiny boy[1]) beside the Avon ;
And closed while Herrick, heedless of the strife
  Of civil war, was singing down in Devon !

[1] "When that I was, and a little tiny boy, &c.
    But when I came, alas ! to wive,
        With hey-ho ! the wind and the rain."

THE LARK.

THE curtains of the East are drawn,
   The sun is looking through,
And hark ! the minstrel of the dawn
   Is up, and at it too !

What gushes of true song are these
   From fountains of the sky
Flung heedless on the morning breeze
   That heedless passes by !

Was ever mortal beauty blest,
   In modern days or old,
With half so sweet salute addrest
   From lover's lips of gold ?

Nay ; but did ever splendour grace,
   Or smiling mirth adorn,
A fairer or a happier face
   Than that of Lady Morn ?

Oh still, where loveliness is had,
   With equal length so long
Will beauty make the minstrel glad
   And gladness run to song !

Thou glorious poet of the dawn !
  What melodies are these
Thou flingest heedlessly upon
  The unremembering breeze?

Could I, in human paraphrase,
  But fix them in a book,
On which in dark and rainy days,
  When thou art dumb, to look—

What harmonies should then be heard
  Of word and note complete !
—With thee, thou little Bird and Bard,
  Not one would dare compete !

———o———

A FIRST OF MAY.

IT was the first of May, and from the town
  Our young folks hastened in their best array,
  Our young folks hastened to bring in the May
From where she loitered on the distant down.
Said one—*I hope she wears her snow-white
    crown;*
  And one—*They heard the cuckoo yesterday;*
  I see her—cried another—*far away*
Like a thin streak of silver on the brown!

So to the down we came, and here and there
  Our little troop went peering far and wide;
Then gathered silent : every bush was bare,
  And snow in the bleak hollows was descried,
And new-born lambs wailed to the wintry air
  Their feeble plaints along the lorn hillside !

———*o*——— .

THE BURN.

WHERE hazel-branches meet o'erhead
  In shade translucent green,
The burn springs from its rocky bed
  And plashes cool between.
It dashes brightly down the den,
  Touched by the morning sun,
And seeks the flat green fields of men
  To have its work begun.

It stays not for the pink wild-rose
  That bends and blushes shy,
Nor for the bank where glittering grows
  The graceful birk-tree nigh,
Nor for the blue-bell, throned a queen
  Amid the strawberry leaves—
For all the beauties of the scene
  It neither stays nor grieves.

It steals one look, in leaping down,
  Towards the distant sky
Where grand and solemn, still and lown,
  The cloudy mountains lie,
Then flings its bright young life along
  The plains that thirsty be,
And rushes in the river strong
  Towards the endless sea!

———o———

ANDRO'S GRIEF.

THE winds, as day was dawning, slept
  After a stormy parley;   ·
And up the sky the laverock leapt
  From out the "mixing" barley,
When Andro from his cottage stept
And looked to heaven, and wept!

I saw his face—his face was pale,
  Tears from his eyes were breaking,
Yet neither sob nor sound of wail
  Told that his heart was aching :
The aching heart—it knows its ail;
But what would words avail?

His little white-haired boy had died
  As dawned the tranquil morning,
And Andro's grief was ill to hide,
  And yet, disclosure scorning,
He hailed me as I passed, and cried—
"A pleasant morning ride!"

———o———

THE SUN'S GOOD NIGHT.

OVER the mountain's shoulder looks
  The Sun to say *Good night*
To all the merry singing brooks
  That sparkled in his light;
To all the dancing waterfalls
  That dashed their diamond spray
Against their green and ferny walls
  In greeting to the day;
To every hill whose gentle breast
  Swells up into the sky;
To every flower that seeks a nest
  Amid the bent so dry;
To all the brave blue-bells that swing
  In every passing wind;
To every bird whose wearied wing
  A resting-place can find;

To quiet sheep that contemplate
  His beams in grassy places;
To children with his smiles that wait
  Upon their chubby faces;
To every tree that glads the glen,
  Sweet birch and rowan ruddy;
To happy wives, and resting men,
  And every other body!

———o———

A TRANSFORMATION.

ALL round a sky of dead continuous grey
  Smothered the valley like a smoky tent,
  Save that a small well-marked irregular rent
In the low roof let in a gleam of day.
All morning to that gap mine eyes would stray
  For the blue freedom of the firmament,
  And with that window I had been content
To gaze afar into the heavens alway.
But suddenly the travelling sun above
  Came to the lattice, and lo! the earth was fair;
The clouds took on the lustre of a dove,
  Twinkled, and flew, and melted into air!
—Such wonders works the smile of one we love
When we are half abandoned to despair!

A DREAM.

O'ERBURDENED with a weight of woes, amassed
  Slowly, I prayed—*Kind spirit, grant a boon :
  Show me that mine's a common care !*—And
    soon
(The present like a mantle from me cast)
I wandered blindfold forward ; till, at last,
  The land of shadows and of shapes unhewn !
  And lo ! the pale face of a frightened moon
Looked on a sea of faces surging past !
And one sad face out of the tidal throng,
  One out of millions, for a moment seen,
Turned round upon me as it swept along,
  And a strange sudden joy altered the mien
—A smile sat on the lips that framed a song,
  And the bright eyes spoke of a faith serene !

——o——

TREASURE-TROVE.

CLIVE, walking down that gallery of gold ;
  A shepherd in the bush, whose staring eyes
  Half doubt the nugget at his feet that lies
From nature's secret treasure-house outrolled ;

A ragged schoolboy, clutching in his hold
  A sudden sixpence ;—vainly memory tries
  Similitudes to make you realise
Her ecstasy : but no ! it can't be told !
—What *was* my find, you ask ?

                 It was the hour
  Friendly to love, when, seeing yet concealed,
Its votaries worship in a twilight bower,
  That, at a crossing, at one step revealed,
Just standing clear of the cathedral tower,
  The new moon argent in an azure field !

——o——

RUS IN URBE.

AMONG the city sounds to-day
  I heard the clacking of a loom,
Or *thought* I heard ; and far away
  My heart went bounding to the broom,
The golden broom ! that to a town
  Whose name to me is ever sweet,
Comes from the hillside tumbling down
  And laughs along the lonely street.

I saw among the fragrant broom
  The herd, a hardy sun-browned elf,

Inhabiting a world of bloom,
  —As once it might have been myself.

I heard the carol of the lark,
  The lyric of the laden bee ;
I saw the silver-glistening bark,
  And tresses of the birken tree ;
The poplars growing by the manse,
  The water bubbling from the well
—How clear as crystal was its glance !
  How musically soft it fell !

I saw the school, the children too,
  The maps upon the schoolroom wall,
The playground—and the white-veined blue
  Of God's protection over all !
The linen bleaching on the green ;
  The basins, shimmering in the light ;
Shrill laughter from a child unseen
  Bringing a searching maid in sight.

I heard the anvil's tinkling sound,
  The smith himself was hid from view ;
I saw the wheel-wright's wheels so round
  Set up in staring red and blue.
The church, the mill, the village store,
  The carrier half-way down the street,
The casks around the grocer's door,
  And Pincher winking in the heat ;

The cottage-windows, bright to view
   With flowers (in pot and box) in bloom
—And all this vision woven to
   The fancied clacking of a loom !—

The sanded doorstep, and the row
   Of haddocks hardening on the wall,
And "bobbin" wives that come and go,
   And spinning-wheels—I saw them all !
And this was in the city street
   With traffic's current pouring strong,
Its black waves weltering at my feet
   And roaring as they rushed along !

Crack ! went a passing cabman's whip,
   —Burst on my ears the world of din ;
The vision gave my mind the slip,
   And all the city hemmed me in !

——*o*——

THE SPRING WOODS.

In life's young ardent prime,
   When winds were soft and skies were blue,
   And spring was making Earth anew,
   These woodlands I have wandered through
   From daybreak till the fall of dew,
Oh many, and many a time !

And now, from foreign clime
  Backward returning with the heat
  Of youth-time gone, I set my feet
  In the old welcoming wood-retreat
  With joy, and hear the birds repeat
With joy the same old rhyme !
Morning and evening chime—
  The same old joys of eye and ear
  Invite me still, and still are dear ;
  And merry schoolboys rambling here,
  As I did whilom fifty year,
Repeat the pantomime !

———*o*———

A SERVICE OF LAMPS.

I woke, and chair and floor were strewn
  With leaves of silver thin,
And at the lattice, lo ! the moon
  Quite close and staring in !

I slept, and woke again, and lo !
  A glory unforetold—
As of a sudden morning glow—
  Filled all the room with gold !

What glorious travelling lamps are these
That o'er my pillow sweep !
—Between their splendid services
Lay just three hours of sleep.

——o——

THE EPILOGUE.

THE season's o'er; sport (save the mark!) is
        poor,
    And on the heather scarcely now remains
    A single gun : already winter rains
Darken and drown the melancholy moor.
And now, where social coveys played secure
    Ere the red Twelfth began, a voice complains,
    To winds that sob in answer, of the pains
The gentle tenants of the waste endure.
It is a plover, wailing through the shade
    Of night and rain-cloud on the upland lea,
Around the marsh, where in the spring it played,
    And piped in summer, with its kindred free
In the bright sunshine.
                    ——Plaints like its have made
The moor a melancholy place to me.

LOCHLEVEN FROM TILLERY HILL.

Look back !—Lochleven, and a rare surprise !
   Long silver lines across its bosom run
   Bright in the light of the September sun :
The rest in purple shadow slumbering lies.
Yonder Benarty, here the Lomonds rise,
   And you may count the islands every one
   —There, in yon castle on the island dun,
Languished Queen Mary, loved of many eyes!—
The scene, though quiet, yet is fair—and full
   Of interest to a guide that knows his trade ;
Chiefly, I must confess, to me (and you'll
   Perhaps endorse the opinion when it's made),
For that Servanus kept his Culdee school
   On yon [1] lone island in Benarty's shade.

——o——

ON READING DR JAMIESON'S HISTORY OF THE CULDEES.

Honour to them who put to rout the dark
   Of Druid rule over our land forlorn,
   What time to lone Iona, ocean-born,
Came through the mists Columba's wandering
     bark !

[1] St Serf's Island.

Honour to them who in a fragile ark
  Nursed the true light amid prelatic scorn
  And papist, till the Reformation morn
At midnight rose from its expiring spark !
Now in these latter times the light again,
  Menaced by controversial mists and blasts,
Grows dim behind the clouds, and purblind
    men
  Follow rush-candles while the tumult lasts :
—But blow, thou clear strong wind of Truth !
    and then
  Shine forth, pure Faith ! on strayed enthu-
    siasts.

——o——

SPRING FROM THE MANSE GARDEN.

Noo owre the weir the watters rin,
  An' skies are saft an' clear,
And infant snawdraps usher in
  The spring-time o' the year.
An' shepherds owre the hills stravaig
  Atween the strips o' snaw ;
An' Pate would noo muil in wi' Meg
  —But Meg begins to thraw.

Noo at the schule, whene'er it skails,
　They gar the peeries bum ;
An' sparrow answerin' sparrow hails
　Frae cottar lum to lum.
—But there are caulds an' yawkin' stogs,[1]
　An' mony a scabbit croon ;
An' Doctor Jalap an' his drogs
　Gang scoorin' thro' the toon !

———o———

PAST AND FUTURE.

In Spring, when hopes like primroses were
　　blooming,
　And youth was in its prime,
'Twas here we talked, our cares to come
　　assuming,
　Like fools, before their time.

We turned our faces from the past so tearless,
　So fresh, and free of stain,
And for the future longed so blindly fearless
　We never dreamt of pain.

[1] Aching stumps : toothache.

D

And now again after a seven years' roaming,
  Under the same green lime,
We almost sigh in the dim summer gloaming
  For that neglected prime.

———o———

AUTOLYCUS AND THE SWALLOWS.

Noo swallow birds begin to big,
  An' primrose-flooers to blaw,
An' Jockie whistles down the rig
  A fareweel to the snaw.
An' glints o' sunshine glancin' gleg
  Licht up the buddin' shaw,
An' wastlin win's are playin' tig
  Roun' ae bewildered craw.

Auld Tammas to the geyvle-wa'
  Nails up a cherry-twig,
An' Mirren watters raw by raw
  Her bleachin' wi' a pig.
An' yonder (he's been lang awa')
  Comes Packie owre the brig,
—An' kintra lads may noo gang braw,
  An' kintra lasses trig.

A LOVE IDYL.

SCENE—*An Orchard.*

Idly roving without aim
Up the orchard path he came,
When, from out a corner cosy,
Stept and stopt him, blushing rosy,
ROSY with her face aflame !

(*He speaks—*)

ROSY ! You deserve your name !
Cheek and chin, and brow and bosy,
—All are of one colour, rosy !

(*A Pause. Then—*)

Is it shyness? . . . Is it shame? . . .
Shall I bless you? . . . Shall I blame? . . .
Ear and eyelid, neck and nosy !
—Was it cherry-brandy, ROSY? . . .
Is't a lover ?

(*A longer pause. No answer. Then—*)

　　　　Here's a game !
Well, I'll stalk him, wild or tame.
No ! you shall not stop me, ROSY !
—Ah ! he's bolted ; yonder goes he !

(*Looking after a retreating figure, her brother
continues—*)

I should know that agile frame . . .
Rosy ! won't you tell his name ?
Come, you'd better !

(*She whispers a name. Then he—*)

Good for Rosy !
Why, he's King of Trumps, is Josey !

——o——

THE COUNTRY LAIRD.

(*Beatus ille, qui procul negotiis,* &c.)

Happy the man who leads the life
   Of patriarch of old,
Far from the city's fevering strife
   And from the race for gold.

He owns with pride his fathers' lands
   —Who would that pride condemn ?
And cultivates with his own hands
   The fields he had from them.

A soldier, when the bugle calls,
  Must leap to meet the foe ;
A sailor, when the storm appals,
  Must hurry from below !

A lawyer.must attend his case,
  His client at his heel ;
A hanger-on, to earn a place,
  Must knuckle down, and kneel.

From fear, and care, and envious hopes,
  The country laird is free,
As to the breezy mountain-slopes
  At morning forth goes he !

How pleasant from their pastoral tops
  To watch his herds below ;
Or see, at mid-day, in the copse
  The oaks he planted grow !

Now in his garden in the cool
  Of shady flowering trees,
He plies an easy gardening tool,
  Or overlooks his bees.

Or on the first warm day in May
  After a genial spring,
He rises at the peep of day
  To view the sheep-shearing.

Or, when the year to harvest comes,
   He stooks the golden sheaves,
Or counts his juicy pears and plums
   And looks in vain for leaves !

While these delightful seasons pass,
   He sometimes may be seen
Extended on the scented grass
   Beneath a leafy screen.

Soft sunshine through the branches peeps,
   And fountains fall around,
And wrens and robins sing—he sleeps,
   Yet hears in sleep their sound.

But Winter comes : the trees are bare,
   The fields are hard with frost ;
And now, you ask, how does he fare ?
   —Are all his pleasures lost ?

See him at early morning, capped
   With fox-fur for the cold,
Step forth, well-breakfasted and wrapped,
   A hardy hunter bold !

On his left arm the shining steel,
   Upon his back the bag,
And sure, but shivering, at his heel,
   Spotty, and Spring, and Shag.

Two red hares in the valley bleed,
　　One blue hare on the hill;
But round the marsh, where wild-fowl feed,
　　There is a deadly *kill!*

Four brace of snipe, a ptarmigan,
　　Six brace of duck and teal,
And, maybe, a fat Iceland swan
　　Fall to the pointed steel.

As homeward in the early gloom
　　A tired man he returns,
He sees far off his dining-room,
　　The fire within that burns;

And, waiting with a welcoming smile,
　　His healthy comely wife
—For an unwedded love's a wile
　　To mar the happiest life.

And now—while *bon vivants* in town
　　Sit o'er their oyster-sauce,
Or gulp the fat green turtle down
　　Their vitiated *hausse;*

Or French ragout, or fricassee,
　　With unclean jaws devour,
Drenching th' unhallowed mixture wi'
　　A claret cold and sour;

Or, maybe, in a lodging-house,
  Or modish restaurant,
They pick their morsel of a mouse
  While still the doors go *bang!*

As black-tailed mutes, bedropt with grease,
  Whisk out, and whirry in,
And bring the biscuit and the cheese
  Before you well begin—

He sits at HIS OWN table-head
  In peace, and plenty too,
And eats his game to home-baked bread
  And native mountain-dew!

One tidy Phyllis, and no more,
  To whom he needs but look,
Receives the dishes at the door
  From a sweet-tempered cook!

He drinks *the Queen, the Church and State,*
  The landed Interest too;
Then, turning to his smiling mate
  —"*And this, my dear, to you!*"

—Oh, that's the life, as all will own,
  Securest yet from sorrow;
I'll sell my shares, call up my loans,
  And buy a farm to-morrow!

. . . . . .

He raised his loans—he realised
Ten thousand for that end ;
A fortnight—and he advertised
Ten thousand pounds to lend !

——o——

A KINTRA SCHULE LADDIE'S LAMENT ON THE LATENESS OF THE SEASON.

(Overheard 19th April 1881.)

THE east wind's whistlin' cauld an' shrill,
The snaw lies on the Lomont Hill ;
It's simmer in the Almanack,
But whan 'ill simmer days be back ?

There's no' a bud on tree or buss,
The craws are at a sair nonplus,
Hoo can they big ? hoo can they pair
Wi' them sae cauld an' wuds sae bare ?

My faither canna saw his seed,
The half o' land's to ploo, indeed ;
The lambs are deein', an' the yowes
Are trachilt wanderin' owre the knowes.

There's no' a swallow back as yet,
The robin doesna seek to flit ;
There's no' a buckie nor a bud
On ony brae in ony wud !

It's no' a time for barefit feet
Whan it may be on ding o' sleet ;
The sizzin's broken a' oor rules—
It's no' the time o' year o' bools ;

It's no' the time o' year o' peeries
—*I* think the year's gane tapsalteeries !
The farmers may be bad, nae doot
—It puts us *laddies* sair aboot !

———o———

MORNING RAINBOW.

In glint and gloom the barley swayed,
  The darting swallow sang,
And sweetly in the gleaming glade
  The bursting blossoms sprang.
As blithesomely I looked along
  Its line of checkered shade,
A rainbow o'er the roadway flung
  A bridge of glorious braid !

The vision stood before I knew,
 And what was earth but lately
(For though it was a charming view
 It did not thrill me greatly)
Became transfigured, grew to me
 Heaven's glorious portal straightway ;
—Expectant I looked up to see
 An angel in the gateway.

———*o*———

THE HAWK AND THE TWO LINNETS.

A HAWK was wheeling in the high hill-air,
 With systematic curve gleaning the heather,
 On the fierce outlook for a partridge feather
Or moor-cock's claw—your hawk loves dainty
 fare—
When, just beneath him, rose a loving pair
 Of linnets, and on social wing together
 Flew jauntily along — they best knew
 whither—
Singing, and of their danger unaware.

He saw, and, ceasing his aerial tour,
 Hung motionless by the sheer strength of
 will ;
Then, like a stone slung with precision sure

And deadly force, meant not to maim but
    kill,
Down came his hawkship, missed, and struck
    the moor;
And those two linnets—they await him still!

—*o*—

THE LAST NIGHT ON THE TOWER.

WHILE to the West the sky is clear,
    Of palest amber hue,
Where warmer tints just disappear
    —The East is purely blue;
The blue of which blue-bells are made,
    As soft as air in Spring,
With here and there a cloudlet laid
    White as an angel's wing.

Down in the vale the village sleeps
    Wrapt in a smoky shroud,
Save where some cottage firelight peeps
    Half frightened through the cloud.
And in the gloom the woody glen
    Seems to contract and close
Its sundered sides to meet again,
    Forgetting they were foes.

The rounded outlines of the hills
  Are carven on the sky;
A star into existence thrills
  And trembles there on high.
Oh fairer than a diamond bright
  Upon a queenly brow,
The first fair jewel of the Night
  Hangs o'er Craiginnan Knowe.[1]

The rushing of the restless streams [2]
  Is surging in the air;
Far up, among the mountains, gleams
  Each fountain, calm and fair.
But ever run the rapid rills
  To seek the Sea's unrest
—And we, too, must forsake the hills
  Upon the self-same quest!

[1] Behind Castle Campbell.
[2] The Care, and the Sorrow—which unite just below
the old castle.

PART III.—SATIRES.

BONES.

THE type is common : there's at least a score
  That look on life as a rare piece of fun
  And all its business a burlesque, for one
That sits and thinks the matter gravely o'er.
You bear with this—you bear it, and deplore ;
  But when in private life you cannot shun
  Nor stop the laughing misery, once begun
—'Tis past all bearing, and the man's a bore !
He comes, and straight up - curls the labial
      sheath,
  Revealing all his dentistry within,
As if the man were God-made for his teeth
  And not to show them were the fatal sin !
Is there no power above (there's none beneath)
  To legislate a close time for the grin ?

NIL NISI MENDACIA!

THEY laud him in the city : seated here
    In sober contemplation, God forbid
    That I should seek to hale what He has hid
From the dead bosom on that lowly bier.
—Yet I will dare to speak and be sincere :
    His life like a smooth-flowing current slid
    And wound through loamy flats; dozing, he did
The easy duty of his narrow sphere.
—But now they deify him ?—That's the wine
    The soups and savoury suppers that he gave :
You may be Divus too, if you incline;
—Give banquets while you live, and, when you
        " cave,"
BROADNOSE will snuffle platitudes divine,
    And GOATLEGS dance devoutly on your grave.

———*o*———

IN SEVEN YEARS.

Seven years ago—only seven years *ago*
    He sat beside me in the Lecture-room
    In all the grace of literary bloom,
And spake of what the *next* seven years would
    show.

Songs, and an Epic, and a Play—but no !
  The Drama was played out : he would assume
  Some strange new form, all radiance and
    pèrfume,
And sling his fancies o'er creation so !
—I stumbled on him near a farm to-day,
  Straws in his hair and hog-wash on his
    sleeves ;
Loud was his voice, dew-lapped his throat, and
  —*Hay !*
  Damn you, the stirks are in among the sheaves!
Amused, but startled more, I turned away
  And left him to his bullocks and his beeves.

—*o*—

KINGS BY DIVINE RIGHT.

NOT these are kings—not these !
  Though girt with gold each brow,
And courtiers on their supple knees
    Before them bow !

Though couriers at the gate
  Await their sealed commands,
To bear the fiat of their fate
    To distant lands !

Though idle throats bray out
  Their *vivats* where they pass,
And helmets compass them about
        With blaze of brass !

Load them with gem and jew'l
  And pearl and purple fine
—Not these, not these the kings that rule
        By right divine !

What ! chosen by the dice
  Of fate—the fault of birth,
Is he, this vicious rake, the vice
        Of God on earth ?

Or tyrants and their tools
  —Does Heaven their crimes ordain ?
By sufferance of their fellow-fools
        The puppets reign !

Who, then, are those that reign
  O'er this terraqueous ball
From East to West and back again,
        Owning it all ?

The Potentates of Thought,
  Of Language and of Lay—
Milton and Shakespeare, Schiller, Scott,
        And such as they !

E

And of the kingly guild
  Are all who feel the flame
Of genius—famed or unfulfilled
            Their dawning fame !

Unmarked they come and go,
  Of outward splendour shorn ;
Yet kings are they without their show,
            And princes born !

Through woods they wander, and
  On lonely hillsides sit,
Too surely conscious of command
            To blazon it !

Yet far as sky is curled
  Or lightnings flash their fire,
They are the kings that rule the world
            By God's desire !

And over all the earth
  Their deathless couriers ride—
Passion and pathos, scorn and mirth,
            And love and pride !

By these they gently sway,
  Enlighten, charm, and bless ;
By these they devastate, and slay,
            Free and redress !

Sceptre nor sword they need,
Nor sense-convincing sign :
They are the kings that rule indeed
By right divine !

————o————

CHRISTOPHER SLY : HIS POLITICAL SENTIMENTS.

THE Peers ! With what complacency they stand
On heights englorified with golden fire !
Look *up*, you tinker !—*look* up, and admire,
And let your grovelling soul with pride expand !
These are the guardians of your native land—
"And they possess it too !" But that's their
hire
For guarding it : all bravery would expire
Unless rewarded with a liberal hand :
Their fathers bled for it—"Get out ! you lie !
Mine fled for it, he did, at Waterloo !"
And they are long descended—"So am I ;
My dad came over with the Conqueror too ;
And what d'ye do for me ? for Christopher Sly ?
—*Gimme a pot of ale, for Godsake do !* '

PART IV.—PSALMS.

O LORD, all things are praising Thee always!
  The mountain's peaceful power; the restless
     sea
  With all its surging music, fiercely free;
The busy rill that stone nor stumbling stays;
The fairy blue-bells swinging on the braes
  In their ethereal beauty born of Thee:
  And with distinctest voice of all does he,
My own belovèd, utter forth Thy praise!
But I, who worship Thee from day to day
  In silence inarticulate, and seek
Passionately to praise Thee, and who pray
  With feeling strong but thought and utter
     ance weak,
Am dumb as are the pebbles of the way—
  Or as an infant, trying first to speak.

SONG OF THE BLADES OF GRASS.

HUMBLE we are and lowly,
  Made to be trodden on ;
Once we had hope, but slowly,
  Softly that hope has gone ;
Yet we despair not wholly—
  On us a star has shone !

When we first woke from sleeping,
  Rose from our earth-bed warm,
Kindly the light came peeping
  Under the tall bent's arm,
And the blue sky seemed keeping
  All on the earth from harm.

But " Here is nought abiding "
  Mournful long grasses say,
Shaking their heads, and hiding
  From us the light of day,
E'en in the sunshine chiding
  If we are glad and gay.

Strange are the things they tell us—
  How can the mighty powers
Ruling the sky be jealous
  Of such a joy as ours?
Sending forth storms to quell us,
  Darkness, and driving showers.

And when the sky is dreary,
 When from the mists the sun
Staggers out wan and weary
 As if his strength were done,
Cry they "'Tis this we fear aye!
 This is our doom begun!"

We are so young beside them
 Withered and old and grey,
We never dare to chide them,
 No matter what they say;
They would have ill betide them,
 We would have good alway.

Surely the skies have heard them
 Murmur in midst of bliss,
And to their wish preferred them—
 To a grey gloom like this—
As in a grave interred them
 Safe from the sunlight's kiss.

Boisterous winds are brawling
 Over the patient hill;
Something upon us falling
 Heavy and damp and chill
Seems to be ever calling
 "Down, little blades, lie still!"

Summer, so long expected,
   Welcome however late !
Come to our hearts dejected,
   Smile on our dismal fate,
Leave us no more neglected
   —It is so hard to wait !

" Patience !" they answer kindly,
   Shadow and shower and breeze—
" Rest in the gloom resign'dly,
   Taking what Heaven may please :
Trust, little children, blindly :
   None of us farther sees."

Yet there was, one morn, lightly
   Hung in our midst, a star !
Glittering and beckoning brightly
   In the high blue afar
—Once we saw many nightly,
   Now know not where they are !

Some of our hopes are blighted—
   Hopes of a summer gone ;
Hopes to be no more slighted
   Trampled, and trodden on :
Yet are we not benighted
   —On us a star has shone !

DISTRUST.

To-day my future seemed too golden clear.
  It cannot be, I said, it cannot be;
  God never meant such happiness for me—
It is not good to have such pleasure here.
Thus medicining my cup of joy with fear
  I sought my window, hoping half to see
  The smiling heaven o'erclouded ominously—
And scared a bird, who thought I came too near.
Ungrateful bird!   It was my hand that spread
  That feast of crumbs for thee, and fleest thou
      thus?
Canst thou not trust the hand that gives thee
      bread?
  Why then so doubtful and so timorous?
—Lord, do we grieve Thee likewise with our
      dread,
  Distrusting all Thy gracious gifts to us?

———o———

THE COMMON CREED.

Lord, with blind eyes we look, and fear;
  We listen with deaf ears, and start;
We think Thou mayst be very near
  —But oh! Thou ever silent art!

And we that would obey Thy will,
  For Thou, we feel, art wise and good,
Search for it in our hearts; but still,
  O Lord, it is misunderstood!

We follow where our passions lead,
  Deeming them lights that lead to Thee;
And when it is Thy light, indeed,
  We think it false, and from it flee!

The soul ignores the human part,
  The human part denies the soul;
To this we lean, from that we start,
  And back again to that we roll!

We weep in hope, we weep in fear,
  Through life's long idly striving day;
And what our hands collect and rear,
  Our hearts destroy, and cast away!

There is no rock on which to rest
  And raise the fabric of a life!
Time with its changes tries the best,
  Long ere oblivion ends the strife!

Yet Thou that mad'st the human heart
  A home of vexing hopes and fears,
—Our Father, not on earth that art,
  Wilt surely one day dry our tears!

IN THE CHURCHYARD AT CHRISTIANIA.

DEATH has no province in the Northern Land,
   To fetter, terrorise with threats, and slay;
   But when he comes (and that late in the day)
He comes, as an official with his wand,
Wearing a bosom-flower and smiling bland,
   To lead the spirit to its rest away.
   Few tears, or none, are shed—not more than
      may
Grace a departure to some distant strand.
They lay the body where they can re-view
   Daily its resting-place : no yew-trees wave
Funereal plumes around of faithless hue,
   A sieve for all the sorrowing winds that rave,
But lightsome blossoms blend their white and
      blue
To make a pleasure-garden of the grave.

———*o*———

AN EVENING HOUR IN ORWELL ACRE.

HERE, in the churchyard by the lake,
One vigil hour I'll gladly wake,
Where Orwell's buried thousands sleep
In social slumber, calm and deep.

Here, while the glooms of evening spread,
I'll sit among the slumbering dead
—No melancholy misanthrope,
Bankrupt of health and heart and hope ;
But full of life, and like to live,
Thankful for joys this earth can give,
A young man drawing cheerful breath,
And yet—no enemy to Death !

I would not have a shortened day ;
And neither would I live alway.
But, since the end I may not know
Of why I live or where I go,
With calm obedience I would wait
The pleasure of omniscient Fate.

'Tis pleasant in the sun to live ;
And Night has her own joys to give.
Our very sorrows and our cares
—The pain they bring us is not theirs ;
Time passes and the pain has oozed,
And now they seem like joys misused.

In calm Eternity's wide view
Little should vex or me or you.
Even Death, which each must undergo,
Whether he bows to it or no,

—'Tis far too common to be sent
Upon us for a punishment.
And I would rather make a friend
And talk of him before the end
Familiarly—keeping the faith
Of all our family with Death.

As thus : I have a canker-care ;
It haunts me here, it hounds me there ;
But *Thou* wilt heal (if none before),
And it will trouble me no more.

A rival ; and he hates me hard,
The harder for my friends' regard ;
Drowning—he would not help me, no !
Yet *drowned*—and he would weep, I know.

We are but boys—fall out and fight,
And cry, and make it up at night,
When *Thou* wilt stroke us on the head
And put us sobbing both to bed.

. . . . . .

How calmly by the mimic deep
The buried crowds of Orwell sleep,
Careless of all that once was dear,
And past the sway of hope and fear !
How enviably long and deep
The buried cares of Orwell sleep !

Night occupies Benarty hill,
The last belated bird is still,
A far-off cottage light goes out,
And darkness gropes the world about !

Save now and then amid the sigh
Of sedges, or the pinewood nigh,
A cushat's low domestic moan,
The worlds of Life and Death are lone ;
Farmhouse and churchyard, lake and hill,
Alike mysteriously still !

Not stiller in the chancel light
Lies the effigies of a knight
Upon the lid of marble stone
He lifts his mailèd hands upon
—His child-meek hands, no more to feel
The pulse of war, the strength of steel—
Than I, upon this green grave-bed,
Rapt into concord with the dead !

I feel, as at the door of death,
My spirit drawing curious breath !

Methinks, though life to me is dear,
'Twere little to die now and here—
To lay upon this turf my head
As on the pillow of a bed,

With this to deepen the delight
That I should have no fears to-night,
And only this to give me pain
That *one* might call on me in vain.

——o——

SONG OF THE CLOVER BLOSSOM.

WITHIN a soft and verdant bed
   Of clover leaves I lie,
While drives the tall grass overhead
   Athwart a cloudy sky.
The wind, that rocks it to and fro
   In agony of pain,
Is whispering soft to me below
   Of pleasant things, and plain.

The long stems, in their anguish, twist
   And bend as low as I ;
Yet see they but the clammy mist
   That makes the fair light die.
Oh, I am poor and small, I know,
   And cannot see so far ;
I only give my scent to blow
   Where no sweet odours are.

I only gaze up timidly
  And wish the light were there,
With no strong cry of agony
  —No heaven-constraining prayer.
I take the sorrow to my heart
  Unshrinkingly and dumb,
And wait till darkness shall depart
  And sunlight's glory come.

———*o*———

SABBATH ON THE HILLS.

O LORD our God, we praise Thee on the height !
  Here in Thy smiling sunshine would we fling
  Earth's mantle from our souls, and let them
      spring
Soaring to Thee, the Father of all light !
From these Thy holy hills their sunward flight
  Nor toilsome were, nor tedious ; on the wing
  Of this pure air upborne, still should they
      sing,
Drawn, praising Thee, from earth to the In-
    finite.
—There are no larks to bless this solitude.
  Silent it lies and looks on the blue sky

Like some great giant, softened and subdued
　By the mild lustre of a loving eye;
Yet, though by angels' song Thine ear is wooed,
　Thou hearest, Lord, the linnet's feeble cry!

———*0*———

A RAILWAY ACCIDENT.

For ever in my memory fast
I see thee as I saw thee last.

—What demon tempts me thus to look
Upon the page of Memory's book,
Where, blurred with blood, with anguish wet,
The annals of that hour are set?
—Heaven from mine eyes in mercy keep
That spectacle that murders sleep!

Surely the pitying angels wept
That should have compassed round and kept
This gentle life that did no harm,
And was of mine the darling charm!

The cruel tragedy is past,
And thou—for ever safe at last!

They shut the door, and locked thee in ;
Good-bye, we said, amid the din
Of bells, and wheels, and gasps that burst
From that black engine's heart accurst !

Good-bye thou saidst—and in my ear
The parting tone yet lingers dear—
While on thy lips there sat the while
A tender, tearful, timorous smile
—As if thou wouldst not seem to part
With boding sorrow in thy heart.

Even now, while sorrowing here I stand,
I feel the tremor of thy hand :
Was it love's tenderness? or fear
—A consciousness that Fate was near ?
Or jar of nerve from shriek and rasp ?
—It was at least our final clasp !

The guard's shrill whistle brought the close,
White steam-balls from the funnel rose ;
Good-byes repeated, friends drew back ;
The engine moved along the track,
Strong and insensate through the gloom,
Deliberately to its doom !

As down the platform passed the train,
I saw thee, Seraph ! once again :

F

The light shone full on eyes and brow
—I saw thee as I see thee now!
O loveliest picture Earth could claim
Set in a carriage window frame!
What radiant beauty from thy face
Lit up the darkness of the place!
It seemed the halo of a saint,
But brighter than the Masters paint,
A glory finer than the sun
—The aureole of Heaven begun!

A moment seen!
           I thank thee, Heaven!
For the clear glimpse that then was given—
It tarried with me from that day,
It tarries with me now alway!

It was as if an angel bowed
Earthward from a dark thunder-cloud,
Then gently, smilingly withdrew
While yet you gazed and ere you knew.

I charge thee, Memory, hold them fast,
Those features as I saw them last,—
Brave eyes, sweet lips, with just a trace
Of transient sadness on the face,
Saintly serenity of brow
—How poor is Earth without them now!

Thou blessèd Angel ! where thou art
Is all my hope, is all my heart ;
And Heaven scarce nearer now can be
Since thou art there to plead for me !

———*o*———

C L O U D S.

THROUGH all the day, in sunshine and in cloud,
  My heart was weighted with prophetic woe—
  " Thus," in the cloud, I dreamt, " will grief
      o'erflow
My smiling plains of joy, and care-weeds crowd
My sunny gardens, by young love endowed :"
  And in the sunshine, " This will shortly go ;
  Let me not trust therein ; too well I know
To none is constant happiness allowed."——
—Whence come these roseate shores that wide
      outroll ?
  Those ebon rocks and flowery islets far
Make with that amber sea a perfect whole.
  To love, all things add beauty ; nought can
      mar.—
The sunset sweeps misgivings off my soul,
  And peace drops from the wings of the first
      star.

HYMN FOR THE NEW YEAR.

O LORD, Thy creatures cry to Thee
    For love, and light, and guidance still !
Their highest hope Thy face to see,
    Their utmost aim to do Thy will.
Thou wouldst not have us vainly grieve
    For faults and follies past and gone?
Be ours the bitterness to leave
    And bear the fuller knowledge on.

From out the ashes of the Old
    The phœnix of the New Year springs
With possibilities untold
    In the proud freedom of its wings.
High may it soar with us, until
    On heights of holiness it dies,
That other years may higher still
    On young unwearied pinions rise!

We drift upon an unknown sea,
    On waves that ever nearer draw
The borders of eternity,
    Obedient to unchanging law.
And through the night we shrink to hear
    On that dim shore their dying fall ;
Till comes the thought to calm our fear,
    That Thou, O Lord, art over all !

TO A FRIEND.

THY work may not be measured; scales and
 rule
 Are for the tangible and transient—thou
 With pain of heart and sweat of brain and
  brow
Pliest thy work with no material tool.
Therefore heed not the rating of the fool,
 Whose blindness to the light would not
  allow
 The glory of the sun that's shining now,
If within walls he circumscribe thy school.

But count thy work in every life that springs
 Attestive to thy teaching, wheresoe'er
On earth it suffers—or in heaven it sings,
 Owning in part its portion to thy care;
And think that round thee may be angel-wings
 As there are hearts, blessing thee unaware!

PART V.

HORACE IN HOMESPUN:

OR,

THE FRIENDS AND FORTUNES OF HUGHIE HALIBURTON,

A SHEPHERD OF THE OCHILS.

————◆————

HUGHIE'S ADVICE TO HIS FRIEN' DAUVIT TO ENJOY THE FINE WEATHER.

Gratia cum Nymphis geminisque sororibus audet
Ducere nuda choros.—CAR. IV. 7.

An' noo ance mair the Lomon'
    Has donn'd his mantle green,
An' we may gang a-roamin'
    Thro' the fields at e'en ;

An' listen to the rustlin'
    O' green leaves i' the shaw,
An' hear the blackbird whistlin'
    Winter weel awa'.

Sae mild's the weather, Dauvit,
   That was but late sae bauld,
We gang withoot a grauvit,
   Careless o' the cauld.

An' juist the tither nicht, man,
   Twa barefit Mays were seen
—It maun hae been a sicht, man !
   Dancin' on the green.

It sets a body thinkin'
   Hoo quick the moments fly,
Hoo fast the days gang linkin'—
   Spring 'll sune be by ;

Then Simmer wi' the roses ;
   Then Autumn wi' the grain ;
Then Winter comes, and closes
   A'thing ance again !

An' yet, tho' short her range is,
   Dame Nature's never dune ;
She juist repeats the changes
   —Juist renews the tune.

The auld mune to her ruin
   Gangs rowin' doon the sky,
When, swith ! a braw bran-new ane
   Cocks her horn on high !

Alas! when oor short mornin'
Slides doon the slopes o' Nicht,
There's nouthir tide nor turnin'
Back to life an' licht!

We fa' as fell oor faithers
Into the narra hame,
An' fowg forgetfu' gaithers
Owre oor verra name!

—But what needs a' this grievin'
For griefs we dinna feel?
Let's leeve as lang's we're leevin',
Lauch as lang's we're weel.

An' if it's guid i' gloamin'
It's better sune than syne
To rise an' gang a-roamin'
Noo the weather's fine!

HUGHIE REMONSTRATES WITH DAVIE,—
A DOUR CRITIC.

*—Si me lyricis vatibus inseres!—*CAR. I. i.

Man, Davie! had I but the ert
To pierce that whunstane o' your hert
Wi' the clear dart o' poesee
—A prooder man there wadna be!

For weel it's kent thro' a' the toun
That nane can rise that ye ca' doun ;
While him that by the haun' ye tak
—He'll nouthir fame nor fortune lack :
His ballants—thro' the touns they'll cry them,
An' lads an' lasses rin to buy them !

There's twa-three praise me, tae, it's true ;
But what are they when wantin' you ?
—'Od, Davie ! but it's hard to tell,
Ye'll maybe praise me yet yersel !

There's Johnnie o' the Windyknowe
—My blessin' on his auld beld pow !
Wi' kindly wird, whene'er he meets me,
He grips me by the haun' and greets me—
"Shackspere !" says Johnnie ; "gie's a swatch o't !
Weel dune, ma bairn ! Ye *have* the catch o't !
That dings the rest ! "—but that's nae test,
For aye wi' him the last's the best.

There's Geordie, tae, my second coushin,
—His praise is waur to me than poushin !
He kens a stirk, but for a sang—
He's never richt but when he's wrang !

There's a fyou mair 'at I could name,—
There's Tam the coo doctor, an' Jame ;

But Jame's my brither, an' for Tam
—Ye'll buy his judgment wi' a dram !

Man, Davie ! if ye would but praise me,
Ye would, as wi' a winlass, raise me
Oot o' the Slough o' Doot I'm in,
An' set me on a road to rin !

Just cast yer een abroad an' see
Hoo everybody's pleased but me—
They've a' some hobby to amuse them,
Folk to look on, an' frien's to roose them,
An' weel contentit there they ride
An' lauch, an' let the wārl' slide !
—An' I an' a' would hae my treasure,
An' poetry would be my pleasure,
If ye would only bend your ee
An' look approval ance on me !

To be a bandsman pleases some,
—To toot the horn or beat the drum.

E'en little Jock, that wirks a mangle,
—Saturday comes, an' the triangle,
An' then sae manfu' as he strides
An' tingles on its iron sides !

An' weel ye ken that Pate Macdougal
Would blaw his sowl into a bugle !

' —That thrice thro' jealousy the wife
O' Dempster poppit Dempster's fife!
An' weel-a-wat the coonty kens
When Sandy Brand ca'd oot the brains
O' his ain fiddle at the fair,
An' swuir he ne'er would fiddle mair
—Altho' he dang'd if he was carin',
Sober he sabbit like a bairn!

Ithers again for days are chammber'd
Wi' hawks' een glowrin' owre a dambuird.

Some at the gowffin' spend their leisure :
To some the rifle-range gies pleasure.

Great was the day when *Dang-your-eyes*
Brocht doun fra Wimbledon a prize!
We rang the steeple wi' a din
That brocht three mile o' the kintra in,
Then at the cross we form'd oor ranks
An' gave oor conquerin' hero thanks ;
We lifted up oor voice on high
An' shouted till we a' were dry.
Then rows an' ale were served aboot
Till ane—fra *hine awa*—cried oot,—
" This tumbler-slockenin' winna *dee*,
There's naething for't but the Brooree!"[1]
—We broke the door, pour'd in haill-sale,
An' a' gat fou on barmy ale!

[1] Brewery.

Quoits an' the puttin' stane hae charms
For steady een an' sturdy arms.
Oh then to see oor noble smith
Tak' up the ball to pruve his pith !
Hark hoo it whizzes thro' the air
—He's foremost by a yaird an' mair !

The slater, tae, ye daurna slicht :
He drave the pin clean oot o' sicht,
An', when wi' shools they howkit for't,
Darkness cam' on, an' spoil'd the sport :
—Nane to this day can understand it,
They howkit but they never fand it !

For me,—gin I had but the ert
To pierce that whunstane o' your hert
Or bring a sparkle to your ee
—A prooder man there wouldna be !
Noo, Davie ! dinna crook your mou !
A wird o' praise is sweet fra you !

HUGHIE DRIVEN IN BY A TEMPEST: HE
DEFIES THE ELEMENTS FROM BEHIND A
JORUM.

—Rapiamus, amici,
Occasionem de die, dumque virent genua.—EPOD. 13.

An angry tempest, roarin' lood,
    Is broken lowse, an' ragin' free ;

The knock-wud groans wi' anguish boo'd,
  An' rocks an' writhes the moanin' sea.
See whaur in whirlin' shooers they flee
The sprays o' ocean owre the main !
  See whaur the leaves o' buss an' tree
Gang streamin' streamin' owre the plain !

Let's tak' occasion frae the day
  To triumph owre a thrawart fate,
An' ere auld age forbid we may,
  Assert oor independent state.
  The win's, that at the window beat,
May tame the tod, an' cowe the craw ;
  But we, wha rank a higher rate,
Will lauch at Winter's wildest law !

Bring oot the jorum—there's a drap
  That should be gurglin' i' the wime o't !
An', while the storm flees owre oor tap,
  We'll toom the cog, an' hae a time o't !
  A cheerfu' quaich—an' whaur's the crime
      o't?
Or aiblins twa—we'll no get fou !
  —'Od ! Rabbie Burns wad mak' a rhyme
      o't
Gin he were here an' saw's the noo !

Hughie's Adventure with a Lion; with a Specimen of Hughie's Inductive Reasoning.

Integer vitæ scelerisque purus.—CAR. I. 22.

An upricht dounricht man like me,
    Whatever chance may happen
In wud or wild, by laund or sea,
    Needs nouthir shield nor wappin !

His lot may be to travel far
    Owre oceans wide an' windy,
Encounter cannibals, or daur
    The fechtin' tribes o' Indy!

But if he's beltit roun' aboot
    Wi' a pure recollection,
He'll fin'—as lately I fan' oot—
    He's in the Lord's protection.

—For but yestreen, as it befel,
    An' I was i' the plantin',
An' juist was sayin' to mysel
    That Tibbie was enchantin';

A lion, that had broken loose
    Fra Wombwell's cam' to try me !

—Though it could 'a torn me like a moose,
  It girn'd, and juist gaed by me !

Put me amang the Sooth Sea Isles
  Wi' cannibals an' cowries,
Or i' the laund o' crocodiles,
  Or e'en amang the Mowries,—

Put me in Africa sae bare,
  Wi' roarin' lions frequentit,
—I'm safe ; an' if my Tibbie's there,
  I'm happy an' contentit !

THE DOG-DAYS : HUGHIE'S EXCUSE FOR A
DRAM.

*Adduxere sitim tempora, Virgili!—*CAR. IV. 12.

An' noo the Dog-days an' their ills
  Come on us frae the Sooth ;
An' we that live amang the hills
  Are a' burnt up wi' drooth.

The kye are stan'in' i' the linns
  Or tiggin' owre the braes,
An' oor wee laddie-herd—he rins
  Skeer naked, wantin' claes !

Cule caller veesions o' the sea,
　　They flit across my brain
Wi' clean white sails an' wun's sae free
　　An' ocean's plouterin' train !

An' no' ae minute wad I stey
　　Could I win owre the door
—It's oh that weary length o' wey
　　Atween me an' the shore !

But you that are beside the sea
　　An' fresh o' wind an' limb
—Your frien' wha canna come to ye
　　—Can ye no' come to him ?

Lay by your oars, an' leave your care
　　Till a' this heat be by,
An' come an' see hoo we folk fare
　　That live by sheep an' kye !

I'll gie ye house-room an' a cooch,
　　My crack an' company tae ;
But *bring a lemon* i' your pouch
　　—It's usefu' aye to hae !

Thae sweet forgaithers are nae crime
　　An' dinna come sae aften :
—It's pleasant at the proper time
　　To spend an hoor in daffin !

HUGHIE HAS A RIPPET WITH TIBBIE.

Felices ter et amplius,
Quos irrupta tenet copula !—CAR. I. 13.

When you, ye jaud,—for say't I maun,
An' little lats that I should bān—
Blink sweetly on anither mān
    Whaur I can see,
Settin' yersel—as weel ye can—
    To anger me !

Then first my hert grows to a lump,
Then bang it goes wi' sic a thump
As nearhan' ca's the vital pump
    Clean aff the hooks,
An' a' my bluid at ae big jump
    Flees to my chooks !

At ither times when i' the street
I hear frae a' the rakes I meet
Yer capers quoted, I could greet
    Wi' grief an' anger,
An' curse yer face, an' voo to see't
    Again nae langer !

Thae bursts o' passion canna bode
A future sanctifeed o' Gōd !

G

Juist cast your een alang the road
  An' see't yersel!
Fechtin' an' flytin'—i' the Lōd,
  It's waur nor, hell!

O three times happy are the pair
Whase bānds o' luve, tho' licht as air,
Nouthir the will o' man can tear,
  Nor will o' woman,
But still they strengthen mair and mair,
  Divinely human!

— .. ...

Hughie expostulates with Marget in behalf o' his neebor Jock.

Lydia, dic.—Car. I. 8.

Marget, my lass, what's this I hear?
  —Jock has been noticed sittin'
Nicht after nicht sin' last New Year
  A' waesome an' begritten.
Nae mair ahint the bothy door
  Is heard his lood guffaw—
An' weel I wat it was a roar!
  —This winna dae ava!

They tell me noo he's never seen
    At herd or horseman stormin',
Puttin' the stane upon the green,
    Or fechtin' wi' the foreman.
Nae langer for the Birnam Games
    He minds to practeese vaultin';
An' a' the kintra grum'lin' blames
    Yoursel for his defaultin'!

When a' the Volunteers were sent
    To face the Queen at Embro',
Puir Jock got mony a sair comment
    Upon his want o' mem'ry.
For when 'twas "Shoulder arms!" they said,
    He thocht on Meg's, an' sabbit;
An' a' the time he hung his head,
    For that had grown a habit.

It gars a body grue to see
    A chiel' sac dowf an' doitet—
It never was the wye wi' me
    To fleech when lassie flyted.
An' weel ye ken that I'm content
    To see ye blithe an' bonnie;
But o' the puir chap's wuts tak' tent,
    For, faith! he hasna mony.

HUGHIE NEARLY KILLED BY THE FALL OF A TREE: HIS REFLECTIONS THEREUPON.

Quam pæne furvæ regna Proserpinæ!—Car. II. 13.

Vow! Wasna that an awfu' crash?
—Wha plantit ye, ill-deedie ash?
As weel doun haudden may he lie
As nearhan' by your fa' was I!
Nane but an ill-designit cratur'
Cud set a tree o' sic a natur'!

He maun hae been an ill-set loon,
A terror to his native toun.
The constable micht wuss to see him—
Nane else, I'm sure :—I wadna free him
Frae takin' aff some simple body
By pittin' pushion in his toddy!

My conscience! But a mawment syne
My breath ye a' but garr'd me tyne.
Ye senseless log, wi' force sae fell,
Ye nearhan' had me like yoursel!
Ye nearhan' got yoursel a name!
—I'll gie ye't yet though, a' the same!

Eh! I was near awa' the noo
Whaur bonnie hazel never grew,

Nor ruddy rowans efter rain   •
Glowed like weet coral doun the den—
A land o' ghaists an' shadows grim,
A' wersh, an' colourless, an' dim !

The waesome strains I micht hae heard
O' mony a lang-forgotten bard ;
They'll wander there fu' dreigh an' dreary,
I'se warrant, wi' their wails sae weary.
An' (may their shades the doot forgie me !)
They michtna hae been gled to see me !

For I wad raither lauch nor greet ;
I canna dae wi' waughts o' weet.
To be a ghaist wad irk me sair
—A mournfu' ane I couldna bear.
But, guid be praised ! I'm no' awa' wi't ;
It hasna been my fate to fa' wi't !

HUGHIE'S WINTER EXCUSE FOR A DRAM.

Deprome quadrimum Sabina.—CAR. I. 9.

Fra whaur ye hing, my cauldrife frien',
    Yer blue neb owre the lowe,
A snawy nicht-cap may be seen
    Upon Benarty's pow.

An' snaw upon the auld gean stump
  Whase frostit branches hang
Oot-owre the dyke aboon the pump
  That's gane clean aff the fang.
The pump that half the toun's folk ser'd,
  It winna gie a jaw ;
An' rouch, I ken, shall be your beard
  Until there comes a thaw.

Come, reenge the ribs, an' let the heat
  Doun to oor tinglin' taes;
Clap on a gude Kinaskit peat
  An' let us see a blaze.
An', since o' watter we are scant,
  Fesh ben the barley-bree—
A nebfu' baith we sanna want
  To weet oor whistles wi'.
Noo let the winds o' winter blaw
  Owre Scotland's hills an' plains,
It maitters nocht to us ava
  —We've simmer in oor veins !

The pooers o' Nature, wind an' snaw,
  Are far aboon oor fit,
But, while we scoog them, let them blaw ;
  We'll aye hae simmer yet !
An' sae wi' Fortune's blasts, my frien',—
  They'll come an' bide at will,

But we can scoog ahint a screen
  An' jouk their fury still.
Then happy ilka day that comes,
  An' glorious ilka nicht;
The present doesna fash oor thumbs,
  The future needna fricht!

HUGHIE'S VIEWS ON WAR.

Nos prœlia virginum
Sectis in juvenes unguibus acrium
Cantamus.—CAR. I. 6.

War's broken oot, an' the toon's wives are
    skirlin',
An' Jock maun awa' to the muster at Stirlin'.

A douce lad, Jock, when he liv'd wi's here,
Stappin' about in his pleuchman's gear,
Or whustlin' blithe on his native braes
—But a deevil to fecht in his scarlet claes!

Nae doot he's braw wi' his sabretache,
An' gluves, an' a swurd, an' a swirlin' mustache,
An' a wee roun' caip on the side o' his pow,
An' his elbows squar'd, an' the drum's *row-dow*

In the swing o' his gang—'Od, a strappin'
    chiel !
Wi' a bricht steel spur like a star at his heel.

But I'm no' at hame in the haunts o' weir,
Wi' its gibbles strange an' its gibberish queer ;
Wi' its *limber* here, and its *aitch-along* there,
Its *parks* and *parades*—an' kens what mair !

I'd like verra weel to descrive it a'
For the sake o' Jock—for he looks sae braw ;
But I micht gang wrang in a wird or a phrase,
An' earn Jock's wrath for the rest o' my days.

The soger-boys are a sicht to see,
But their style o' fechtin's no' for me—
Wi' their blawin' ye up, an' their ca'in' ye roun',
An' their stickin' ye dead when they get ye
    doun !

The only fechtin' *I* care aboot
Is when a Meg wi' her jo fä's oot :
She lowses upon him a tinkler jaw
An' rugs his hair ; an' he bears it a'
—An' it's a' made up in an hoor or twa !

HUGHIE'S ASTONISHMENT ON HEARING THAT
HIS YOUTHFU' FRIEN' WULL, A QUATE
STUDENT LAD, HAS RUN OFF TO THE
SOGERS.

Cum tu coëmptos undique nobiles
Libros Panæti, Socraticam et domum
Mutare loricis Iberis,
Pollicitus meliora, tendis?—CAR. I. 29.

Wull, ma bairn ! what's this o't noo?
    Here the wird gangs that ye're listed !
I declared it wisna true,
    But they threepit and insisted :——
Sae ye think to mak' a steer
I' the weary warl' o' weir?

Are ye gaun to fecht the Booers,
    Or the Zulus an' the Caffirs?
Or defy the Allied Pooers
    For a wheen o' guizened gaffers?
Ye'll be gaun to set them strecht,
Ay! an' shaw them hoo to fecht !

Eh, man ! tho' the tranquil Tay
    Roared in spate wi' sudden thunner
On a cludless simmer day
    In a drouth—I wadna wunner !

Naething noo can startle me
When a lad like you's sae ree !

We were blawin' lang an' lood
  O' your pairts an' o' your knowledge ;
Eh ! the minister was prood
  When he got ye sent to College !
—This is a' ye're makin' o't,
Prancin' in a scarlet coat !

HUGHIE'S ADDRESS TO A JILT—WITH A POSTSCRIPT OF REFLECTIONS.

*Cui flavam religas comam ?—*Car. I. 5.

Weel, Mysie ! wha's the favoured noo
  To tryst wi' ye at e'en ?
—He'll be the dentiest chield, I troo,
  That ever yet ye've seen.
Ye'll wander by the breery brae—
The roses *you*, the thorns *he* 'll hae—
An' sair, puir man, he'll feel the spell
That mony a day I did mysel.

Nae doot your bonnie yellow hair—
  I ca'd it gowd langsyne—
He'll praise wi' sic anither air
  An' flatterin' speech as mine. . . .

—Puir fallow !   She's a' smooth the noo ;
But bide awee till meets his view
A veesage thrawn wi' peevish spite,
Dorty an' dour, 'ill drive him gyte !

I peety him wi' a' my heart,
   The puir bit silly cratur' !
It's gled he'll be frae her to pairt
   When ance he kens her natur'.
Only for his escape I grane
Wha am sae joyfu' in my ain ;
For blithely do I bless the hoor
That saw me safe beyond her pooer !

HUGHIE'S SPRING SUNSHINE DASHED WI'
SHADOW.

Solvitur acris hiems grata vice veris et Favoni—

Vitae summa brevis, &c.—CAR. I. 4.

The winter ice is breakin' up,
The wast wind whustlin' cracks his whup,
An' noo ye hear their *Hi-wo-hup !*
     —It's worth the hearin'—
As pleuchmen lads wi' steady grup
     Draw oot their feerin'.

An' noo ere lang we'll see the flooers
Drawn fra the divots by the shooers,
An' saft win's hing the plantin' booers
    Wi' leaves that rustle,
An' laricks to the lift a' hoors
    Flee up, an' whustle !

It's braw an' blithesome i' the spring
To see the joy o' everything ;
Dance, bairns an' bodies, dance an' sing
    —Ye dae't wi' reason :
Whatever joyous thocht ye bring,
    It comes in season !

Dance while ye can—sing while ye may,
For human life's a short-liv'd day ;
—Owre sune, owre sune the gloamin' grey
    Creeps cauld athort it,
And we in death oor limbs maun lay
    Where late we sported !

Hughie's advice to Tammy to live less for the future and more for the present.

Nec Babylonios
Tentaris numeros.—CAR. I. 11.

Gie owre thae wuld uncanny looks,
That trokin' wi' the deevil's books,
That doctorin' o' yoursel wi' simples—
It only fills your face wi' pimples—
An' learn to live like ither folk
Whase trust is in their aitmeal-poke !

Ye winna grow ae bit the stranger,
Ye winna live ae hoor the langer,
For a' your cairds an' calculations,
Your auld witch-wifie consultations,
Your herbs an' drogs, yer drinks an' plaisters,
An' a' your ither stinkin' slaisters !
You'll live nae langer, an' nae less,
Than a' your days—ye maun confess.

Dootless ye've heard o' Doctor Faust
—*He* brewed himsel a bonnie browst !

But surely it's the manlier gate
To wait wi' patience on your fate ;—

To sup your parritch, tak' your smoke,
An' dee at last like ither folk?
This eager wish o' yours to scan
The future, an' prolong your span
—It's fār frae gude, it's doonricht bad,
Half irreligious, an' half mad!

What better would ye be to ken
Hoo mony years ye've yet to spen'?
—For past the boon's ye couldna lengthen't,
An' what there's o't ye couldna strengthen't!
Ye'd only live a life dementit,
An' dee alane an' unlamentit!

Tammy, my man! tak' my advice,
An' follow't, an' we'll ca' ye wice!
Draw in your hopes, an' keep your fears
Commensurate wi' your mortal years;
Enjoy the present—crack your joke,
An' tak' your dram wi' sober folk!
Gie owre—tho' I should tire your patience—
Gie owre thae lang anticipations!
They pushion a' the passin' hoor
An' turn a sweet intil a soor!

An' a' this sacrifeece for what?
Juist think, afore ye answer that.
Noo! answer fair, an' I'll be dumb:
—*A future that may never come!*

HUGHIE'S THOUGHTS ON LOVE, SUGGESTED BY SANDIE'S PLIGHT.

Sic visum Veneri, cui placet impares
Formas atque animos sub juga aënea
Sævo mittere cum joco!—CAR. I. 33.

Hoot, Sandie ! this 'ill never dae !
Ye're juist a perfeck winnlestrae—
   Ye're no' a man ava !
Look up, an' see the licht o' day
   Afore yer gloamin' fa' !

Tho' Bess, sae proper an' perjink,
Ne'er deigns on ye to cast a blink
   For a' ye're like to dee—
Ye're no' alane, ye needna think
   —Look roon' ye, an' ye'll see !

For ane, that puir bit lassie, Bell,
Thinks mair o' Allan than hersel,
   An' *ony* gate she'd gae wi' 'im !
He's juist as daft for saucy Nell,
   An' *she'll* hae nocht to dae wi' 'im !

—This warld's jummled a' throuither !
An' noo we staund as in a swither,
   On ithers' folly thinkin' ;
An' noo we tig wi' ane anither,
   An' miss oor mates wi' jinkin' !

For (in yer lug) juist look at me !
Blithe Jenny withoot ae bawbee
    Has a' my wuts discardit ;
While Nance, wi' tocher fair an' free,
    Smiles sweetly unregardit !

HUGHIE JILTED AGAIN : HE DERIVES CONSOLATION FROM PROPHECY.

Ast ego vicissim risero.—EPOD. 15.

I mind the place, I mind the hoor
—It was ahint the castle tow'r
Just as the mune wi' muirlan' glow'r
        Rase owre the plantin,'
An' hoolets blinkin' frae their bow'r
        Begoud their chantin' !

Aroond my neck ye flang your airms,
An' swore by death an' ither hairms
Henceforth to dedicate your chairms
        Alane to me !
I wadna, no ! for fifty fairms
        Niffered that lee !

For lee it was !   Within a week
Willie, the hauflin', gat a keek

An' saw ye lift your perjured cheek
      To Wabster's mou'!
An' heard ye in a whisper speak
      The self-same voo!

But bide awee! the time'll come
At him an' a' ye'll tak' a strum!
Then back to me!—But I'll be dumb,
      Or bid ye gae!
An' ye, wha thocht yoursel a plum,
      I'll coont a slae!

Wabster, my man! a word to you!
—The hoor's at hand when ye'll alloo
That never limmer mair untrue
    .   Cam' to the clachan :
Then ye'll be dowf an' doun i' mou',
      An' I'll be lauchin'!

HUGHIE BIDS FAREWEEL TO LOVE.

Tange Chloën semel arrogantem.—CAR. III. 26.

I'm dune wi' love for ance an' a'!
—Nae mair noo at the gloamin's fa'
I'll wash my whuskers, redd my hair,
An' busk my craig wi' muckle care,

Syne, whustlin' up some amorous ōd,
Oot wi' my staff, an' to the road !

Nae mair wi' pain I'll warstle thro'
Nettles and breers an' thorns to pu'
A posie for some bonnie May,
Whase smile micht maybe last the day,
—But when the morn again ye met her
She'd be ta'en up wi' some ane better !

An' never mair I'll praise again,
In simple sang o' soothin' strain,
Deep-dimpled chin an' cherry mou',
An' locks wi' sunlicht blinkin' thro',
—Nor saft blue een, nor black, nor broun:
I've haen a turn o' them a' roun' !

Sonnets an' sangs, I lay them by
Whar' a' my youthfu' memories lie ;
My Sabbath braws, the coat-tail pocket
Wi' keepsake flooers an' favours stockit ;
Sweeties ; and a' the ither arts
I've tried—to win the lassies' hearts !

But ere I gie't up a' thegither
Grant me a conquest owre *ae* ither,
You that wi' bended bow are lauchin'
To hear us wi' your arrows scrauchin'—
I've haen my day, I've haen the maist o't,
—Gie saucy Tibbie noo a taste o't !

HUGHIE OFFERS HIS CONSOLATIONS TO HIS
SISTER MEENIE, WHASE HEART IS WI'
DONALD IN LOCHIEL.

Miserarum est neque amori dare ludum neque dulci
Mala vino lavere, aut exanimari metuentes
Patruæ verbera linguæ.—CAR. III. 12.

'Od, Meenie, but I'm vexed for ye!
—A lad could better thole, ye see,
   The pains o' love unspoken ;
For he could speak—an' he could pree
   A gless, hooe'er heart-broken !

But you, puir wumman ! need to bide
Tongue-tied aboot the ingleside,
   Baith dowff an' dowie, hearin'
Girnin' auld Nance, as gleg as gley'd,
   Your ailment sweetly speirin' !

—'Deed, Donald is a stately chiel' !
There's no' a gamie in Lochiel
   Sae brisk-like or sae daurin' ;
Gin ye should wale a lad, atweel,
   Ye micht hae waled a waur ane !

The loch he'll soum to conquer there
The stag that stan's in fierce despair
   'Mang seggs, sae eerie soughin' ;

He'll rouse the wul'-cat frae her lair
To mak' o' her a spleuchan !

Nae doot he *is* a wiselike lad :
But mony as gude are to be had ;
  An' ye maun mind, my dawtie,
Tho' Nance is an ill-natur'd jaud,
  Ye've been a wee thing fauty.

Whan dreigh an' drearie doun ye sit,
Up wi' your wires, an' knit, an' knit,—
  Ye'd wonner, withoot jokin',
Hoo muckle ravell'd care ye'll pit
  Awa' into a stockin'.

HUGHIE AS A PHILOSOPHER : HE ENFORCES THE GOLDEN MEAN.

Auream quisquis mediocritatem
Diligit.—CAR. II. 10.

The course a gude sailor wad haud at the sea
Is neither owre muckle to win'ward nor lee,
For on this side's the tempest, on that are the
  rocks
—But he steers straucht atween an' keeps clear
  o' a' shocks.

Noo that's juist the mean ye should follow on
    land :
—The wun's 'ill wage war wi' your castle sae
    grand ;
Your puir cottar-hoose they'll ding doun a'
    thegither;
—Ye shouldna seek aither the tane nor the
    tither !

The fir on the hill-tap maun weather the storm,
Maun face the fell winter in terriblest form ;
The gress on the plain maun be trampled and
    trodden,
Wi' spates an' wi' rains be disfeegur'd and
    sodden.

Ye're baskin' i' sunshine, yoursel and your
    hoose?
Weel, a' body's no'—mind that an' be douce !
An' gin ye hae ever o' troubles your fill,
Think some are waur aff an' ye'll no' be sae ill !

The haund that brocht on ye the cauld and the
    snaw—
The same, wi' ae waff o't, 'ill tak' them awa ;
Then binna perplext, but tak' a' wi' a mind
That's brave when it's patient, an' wise when
    resign'd.

HUGHIE IN MURNINS : HE LAMENTS THE LOSS O' HIS FRIEN' ANDRO.

Ergo Quinctilium perpetuus sopor
Urget !—CAR. I. 24.

What man or minister 'ill dare
Haud oot his haun' an' cry—*Forbear !*
This wild, this waefu' sorrow spare ;
It's Nature's debt !
—But I will band an' weepers wear
For Andro yet !

O for the wail o' autumn wun's,
An' trees, an' seas, an' settin' suns,
An' melancholy muirland whuns
An' hillside sadness !
O for the greetin' voice that runs
Thro' Nature's gladness !

So Andro's gane ! .The lang last sleep
Has fa'en upon him, an' he's deep !
An' noo he disna hear a cheep
O' a' we're taulkin' !
An' we in vain oor watch wad keep
For him to wauken !

It's no' the stroke, tho' fell an' grim,
The bosom cauld, the moveless limb,
That melt an' mak' oor een sae dim,
      Oor herts sae sair—
But oh ! what virtues sleep wi' him
      That's lyin' there !

He was sae modest an' sae true—
Truth was engraven on his broo !
Strict wi' himsel, an' slack wi' you,
      An' even-mindit—
His peer, search a' the warl' thro',
      Ye winna find it !

An' noo he's gane ! he's crost the mark
Atween us an' that ocean dark
Whauron some day oor ain frail bark
      Maun sink or sail !
—But here nae mair we'll hear or hark
      His kindly hail !

HUGHIE MAKES IT UP WITH TIBBIE.

Rejectæque patet janua Lydiæ. —CAR. III. 9.

HE.

The days afore we disagreed
   When you were sweet an' kind—
Ah! *thae* were happy days, indeed ;
   They'll never leave my mind !

SHE.

They would been happy yet, say I,
   Had ye been kind an' true :
That e'er thae happy days gaed by
   Was a' the faut o' you !

HE.

Ye maunna think frae what I've said
   That it's a' owre wi' me—
There lives in yonder manse a maid
   I'm juist as happy wi' !

SHE.

An' dinna think that *I* am sad
   Or would to grief incline—
There waits in yonder loan a lad,
   I'm blithe to ca' him mine !

HE.

But, maybe, if I left the maid,
  —Tho' *that* would gie me pain !—
Maybe ye wouldna shake your head,
  But tak' me back again?

SHE.

O ye're a fickle faithless chiel',
  As fause as ever spak',
Yet weel ye ken I'm yours, an' weel
  Ye ken ye're welcome back !

THE CRITIC AT LAST RELENTS : HUGHIE AS AN EAGLE !

Jam jam residunt cruribus aspera !—CAR. II. 20.

What, Davie ! d'ye say't o' me
That I'm a bard an' born to flee ?
—I doot it's juist a bonnie lee
    That ye've inventit !
—Na ! if ye threep it, it maun be ;
    But ye maun prent it !

I wunner whatna bird I'll be !
—'Od, if the choice be left to me,

I'll be an eagle ! Wha but he
  To rule the air !
The verra sun wi' open ee
  He can ootstare !

His flicht is owre the cludds o' heaven
—He screams abune the flashin' levin
That sends the wee fools terror-driven
  Hame when they see't !
The heichest hills are thunder-riven
  Aneath his feet !

Nae peer has he ! an' wha wad daur
The rushin' o' his wings in war?
Or seek wi' impious bolt to bar
  His plumaged pride?
Nae fear has he ! his flicht is far,
  His empire wide !

—Already doun my sides I feel
The feathers creepin' ! on my heel
Twa spurs stick oot as sharp as steel !
  My wings are risin' !
I'm ready for the lift ! fareweel !
  I'm aff, bird-guizin' !

Wi' ae waff o' my wings I soar
A mile abune the city's roar—

Then roun' the warl', shore efter shore,
  Wi' pinions regal
I flee a strang flicht wi' the core,
  A brither eagle !

Homer flees first—for wha wad seek
To tak' that honour fra the Greek ? ˙
Then Pindar wi' triumphant beak
  An' bluidy talons
—Tho', whyles, he whummles wi' a shriek
  Clean aff his balance !

Then comes a lower flicht—but still
Far far abune oor heichest hill ;
Yon's Virgil wi' his weel-preen'd quill,
  An' this is Horace ;
—A band o' eaglets screamin' shrill
  Mak' up the chorus !

But wha is this wi' brunt ee-bree
An' scowther'd on the wings awee ?
It's Dante : he delights to flee
  A' by himsel.
The fire that's in his flamin' ee
  He stole fra hell !

An' yonder, noo, ye may descry
Shakespeare an' Milton ridin' by,

Dimmin' the haill dome o' the sky,
 Their ain dominion;
While far—far—far aneath them, I
 Streek oot my pinion!

But yet it's graun' to sail the air
Altho' a mile below the pair;
To flap yer wings owre earthly care,
 Owre kirk an' steeple,
An' see them point *lo here! lo there!*
 —The gapin' people!

Nae mound nor monument for me
—An eagle-poet canna dee!
But when the lichtnin' flashes free,
 The tempest sings,
—Look up! an' in the tumult see
 My eagle wings!

PRINTED BY WILLIAM BLACKWOOD AND SONS.

ORELLANA,

AND OTHER POEMS.

By J. LOGIE ROBERTSON, M.A.

Fcap. 8vo. Printed on hand-made paper, 6s.

" He has tender love-songs, outbursts of cynicism and satire glowing word-pictures of natural scenery, and clever studies of rhythm and metre,—all of them characterised by a very distinct individuality and artistic facility."—*Scotsman.*

" Many have a sub-humourous tone. In this Mr Robertson seems to excel. 'A Gift for a Bride' seems to us particularly good."—*Spectator.*

"The talented author has a fine eye for nature, and can describe its varying scenes with a freshness, a truthfulness, and often with a brilliancy which enchain the attention and positively extort admiration."—*Edinburgh Daily Review.*

" Is full of fire and vigour."—*Whitehall Review.*

"Displays an originality that constrains the most earnest attention, and awakens sensations even in the case-hardened critic of unalloyed delight.......They offer a rich variety, both as to tone and treatment. Graphic portraiture both of human character and natural scenery, spiritual insight, pathos, and humour,

will be found in them........If it were only for its exquisite interpretation of the northern scenes with which we are all familiar—though that is but one of its merits—we should have no hesitation in giving Mr Robertson's book a high place among the very best productions of the modern Scottish muse.......
He can be as nimble, neat, and dainty in his lighter moods as any Dobson or Locker; yet he ascends to heights which the choicest of these writers could not by any possibility reach, and no matter how high he soars, he remains as spontaneous and single as in his humblest lilt.......The poem (Orellana) will be read through- at a sitting by every one who begins it."—*North British Daily Mail.*

"'From the Sicilian of Vicortai' is the title above a small collection of beautiful and delicate verses. We presume that it is Sir Theodore Martin who has given us the pleasure of meeting such beauty in so fair a dress. The style has near kin to the dream-wrapt passion of Heine, and the measure flows as if Poe had come to sing from his tomb."—*Greenock Advertiser* (in review of 'Blackwood's Magazine' for December 1880).

"The story is told with poetic grace, and many of the tropical scenes are represented with a warmth of colouring which only a poet can give."—*Dundee Courier.*

".....Mr Robertson whose touch is so delicate, and whose fancy is so graceful.......Plenty to read, to re-read, and thoroughly to enjoy."—*Sunday Times.*

"'From the Sicilian of Vicortai' is throughout marked by tenderness and elevation of sentiment, and no little melodiousness of verse."—*Aberdeen Free Press.*

WILLIAM BLACKWOOD & SONS,

EDINBURGH AND LONDON.